BOATS

Speeding! Sailing! **Cruising!**

by Patricia Hubbell

illustrated by Megan Halsey and Sean Addy

Marshall Cavendish Children

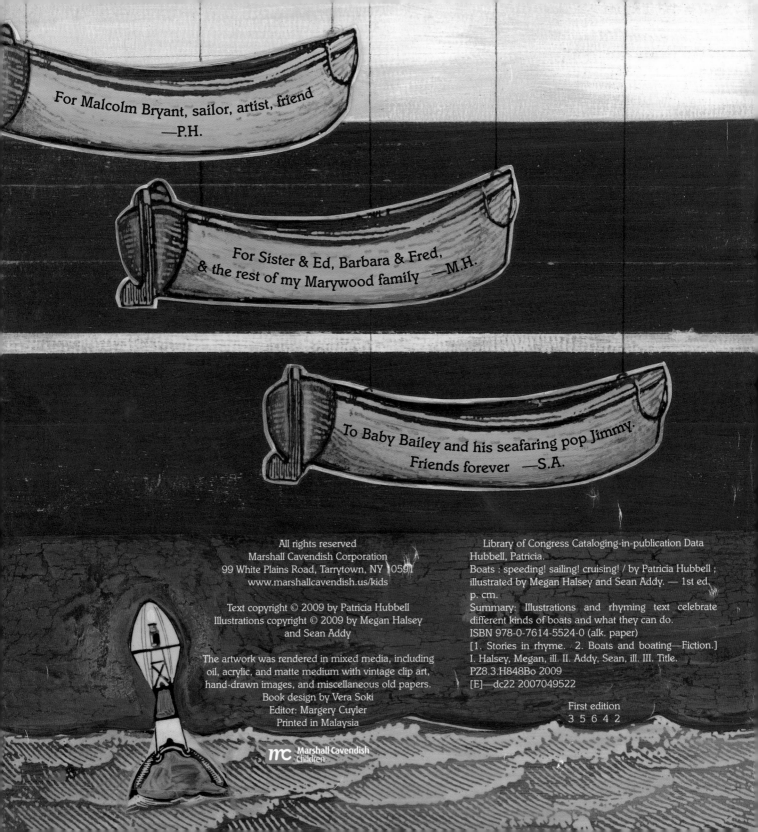

For Malcolm Bryant, sailor, artist, friend
—P.H.

For Sister & Ed, Barbara & Fred,
& the rest of my Marywood family   —M.H.

To Baby Bailey and his seafaring pop Jimmy.
Friends forever   —S.A.

Text copyright © 2009 by Patricia Hubbell
Illustrations copyright © 2009 by Megan Halsey
and Sean Addy

The artwork was rendered in mixed media, including
oil, acrylic, and matte medium with vintage clip art,
hand-drawn images, and miscellaneous old papers.
Book design by Vera Soki
Editor: Margery Cuyler
Printed in Malaysia

Library of Congress Cataloging-in-publication Data
Hubbell, Patricia.
Boats : speeding! sailing! cruising! / by Patricia Hubbell ;
illustrated by Megan Halsey and Sean Addy. — 1st ed.
p. cm.
Summary: Illustrations and rhyming text celebrate
different kinds of boats and what they can do.
ISBN 978-0-7614-5524-0 (alk. paper)
[1. Stories in rhyme. 2. Boats and boating—Fiction.]
I. Halsey, Megan, ill. II. Addy, Sean, ill. III. Title.
PZ8.3.H848Bo 2009
[E]—dc22 2007049522

First edition
3 5 6 4 2

mc Marshall Cavendish
Children

Boats! Boats! Boats!

Big boats. Snug boats—
tough, hardworking tugboats.

Yachts with flags both fore and aft.

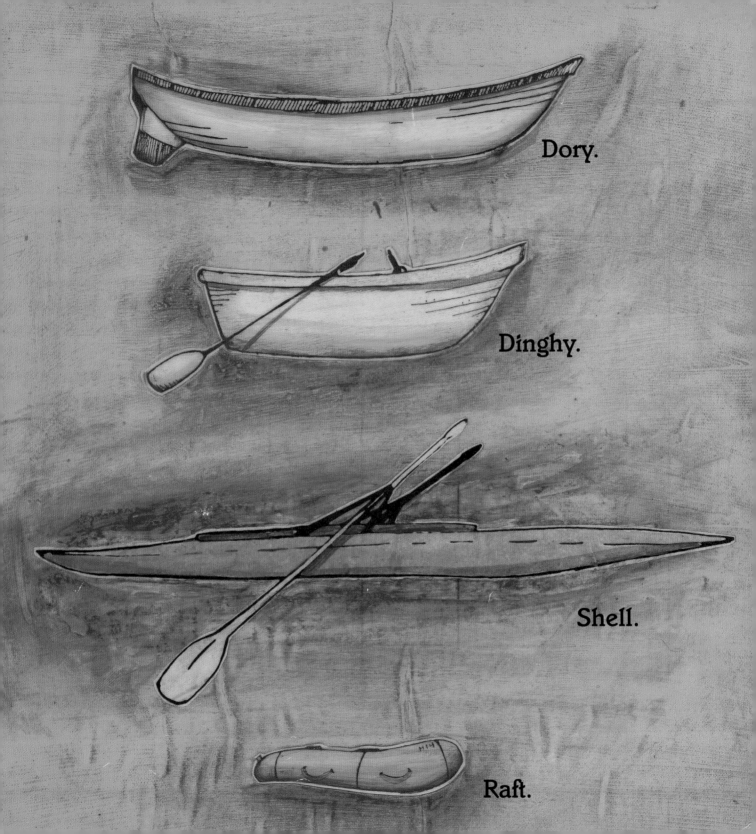

Dory.

Dinghy.

Shell.

Raft.

Catamaran. Bark canoe.
Kayaks made for one and two.

Boats for families and their pets.

Trawlers with enormous nets.

Lobster boats. Whale boats.

Tossing-in-a-gale boats.

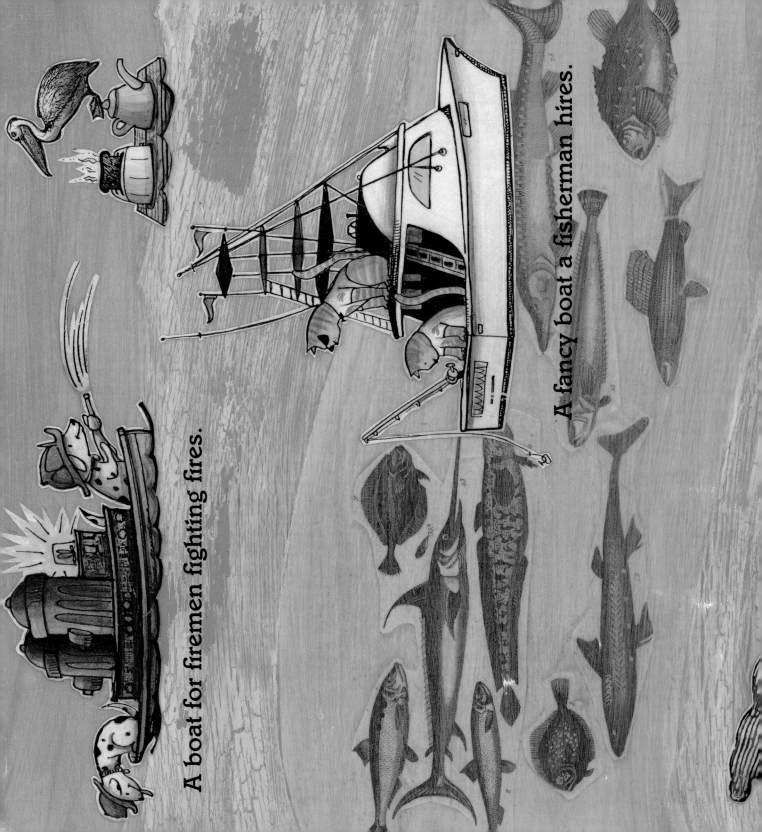

A boat for firemen fighting fires.

A fancy boat a fisherman hires.

Big barge hauls a load of steel.

Showboat churns its paddle wheel.

Rumble! Whistle! Roar! Toot!
Chug! Hum! Sputter! Hoot!

Rev the engines! Speed ahead!

salon

deck

engines

Deck. Cabin. Galley. Head.

galley

deck

head

cabin

Ferries with their decks packed tight
ply the seas both day and night.

Icebreakers smash an icy floe;
penguins dive down deep below.

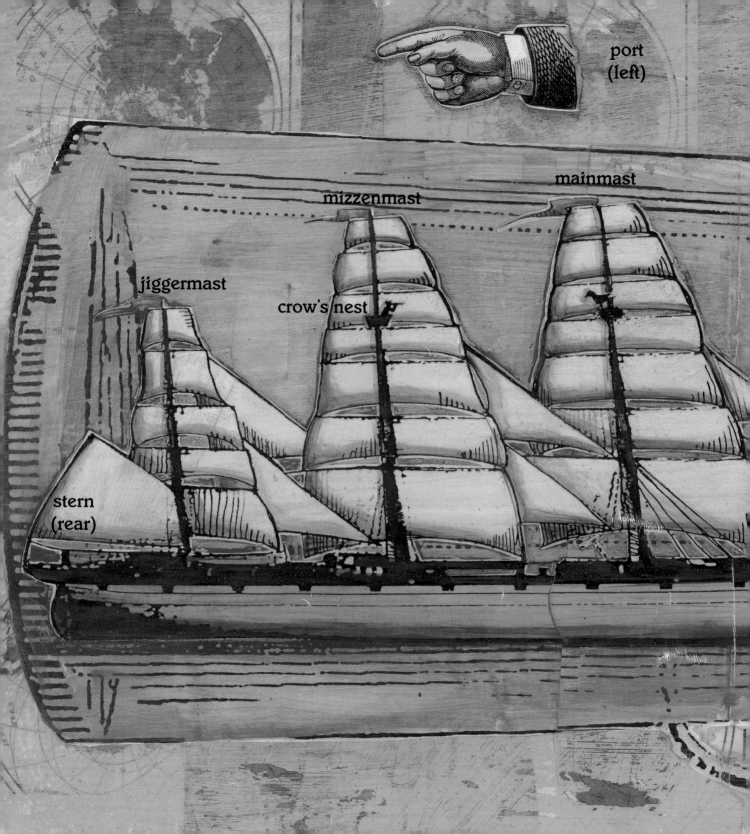

port
(left)

mainmast

mizzenmast

jiggermast

crow's nest

stern
(rear)

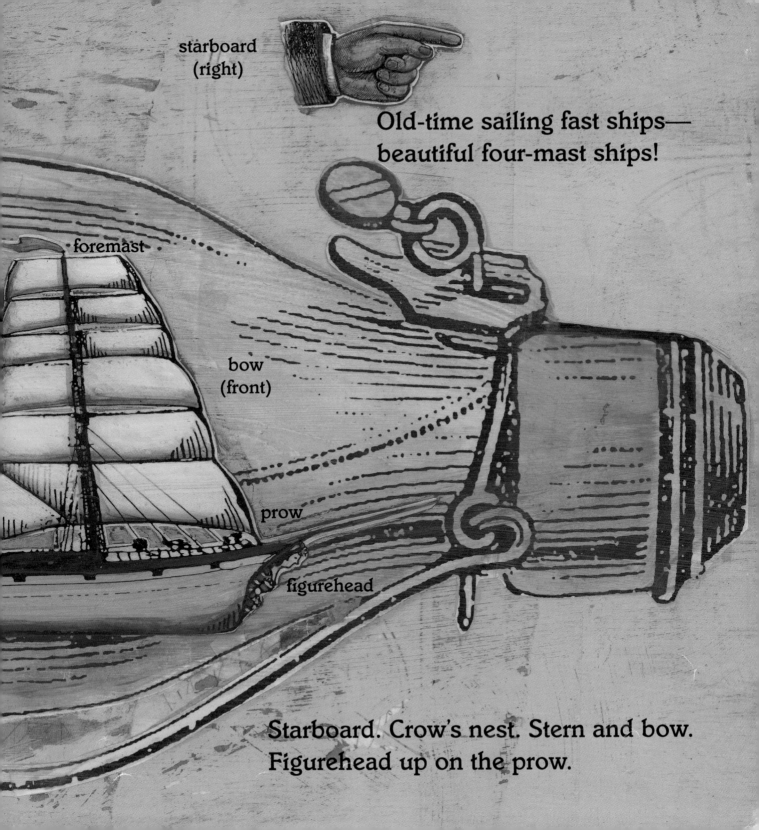

starboard
(right)

Old-time sailing fast ships—
beautiful four-mast ships!

foremast

bow
(front)

prow

figurehead

Starboard. Crow's nest. Stern and bow.
Figurehead up on the prow.

Liner. Cruise ship. Tropical shore.
Down the gangplank. Let's explore!

chief engineer

chief steward

MENU

A great big ship needs
a great big crew.

first mate

radio operator

Everyone has lots to do.

Fighting ships of the U.S. Navy
plow through seas, wild and wavy.

ALL-AMERICAN

Cruiser.

Battleship.

Submarine.

And the biggest ship you've ever seen . . . .

An aircraft carrier where pilots fly
planes that zoom into the sky.

Toy boats sail in
ponds and streams,

in your tub
and in your dreams.

To: The North Pole

To: The West Indies

To: The East River

Boats sail north, south, east, and west.

They do their jobs.

To: South of the Equator

Then they rest.